LOCH NESS
Monster

by Marie Pearson

raintree

a Capstone company — publishers for children

Raintree is an imprint of Capstone Global Library Limited, a company incorporated in England and Wales having its registered office at 264 Banbury Road, Oxford, OX2 ?DY - Registered company number: 6695582

www.raintree.co.uk
myorders@raintree.co.uk

Editor: Claire Vanden Branden
Designer: Becky Daum
Production Specialist: Laura Manthe
Originated by Capstone Global Library Limited

ISBN 978 1 4747 8766 6 (hardback)
ISBN 978 1 4747 8776 5 (paperback)

British Library Cataloguing in Publication Data
A full catalogue record for this book is available from the British Library

Acknowledgements
We would like to thank the following for permission to reproduce photographs: Alamy: Elena Babenkova, 20–21, Science History Images, 14–15; iStockphoto: AndrewJShearer, 24–25, brytta, 12–13, FotoGraphik, cover, gremlin, 23, Lensalot, 5; Newscom: Pictures From History, 6, The Print Collector Heritage Images, 11; Shutterstock Images: dnaveh, 18–19, Lukassek, 26–27, 29, Mike H, cover, Roman Babaki, 17, Thanakorn.P, 30–31, Victor Habbick, 8–9, 28
Design Elements: Shutterstock Images, Red Line Editorial

Every effort has been made to contact copyright holders of material reproduced in this book. Any omissions will be rectified in subsequent printings if notice is given to the publisher.

All the internet addresses (URLs) given in this book were valid at the time of going to press. However, due to the dynamic nature of the internet, some addresses may have changed, or sites may have changed or ceased to exist since publication. While the author and publisher regret any inconvenience this may cause readers, no responsibility for any such changes can be accepted by either the author or the publisher.

Printed and bound in India.

CONTENTS

CHAPTER 1

A DEADLY Monster

Loch Ness is a loch in the Highlands of Scotland. People have told tales of a monster beneath the surface. The first story was first told many years ago.

It was 22 August in AD 565. A **monk** called Columba wanted to cross the River Ness. The river Ness flows from Loch Ness. Columba waited with other men. No one had a boat.

Then Columba saw a group of people with a man. The man was dead. They said there was a big monster in the water and it had killed him.

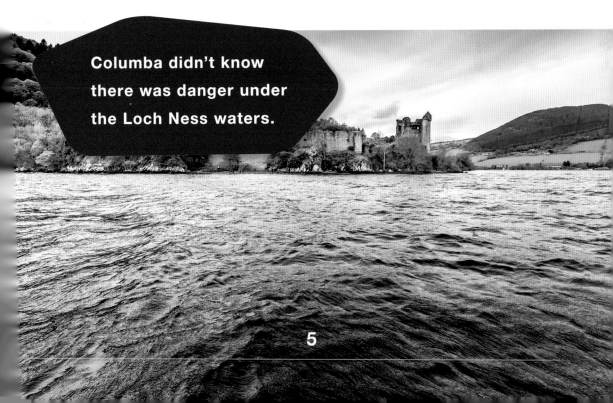

Columba didn't know there was danger under the Loch Ness waters.

Columba saw a boat across the loch. He asked another man to fetch it. The man dived into the water and began to swim. But the monster heard him. It roared. It opened its mouth wide and sped towards the man.

LOCH NESS

Loch Ness is 36 kilometres (23 miles) long. It is 240 metres (788 feet) deep. It is the second-deepest loch in Scotland.

The monster was only a few feet away from the man. Columba signed a cross in the air. He commanded the monster in the name of God. He told it to leave the man alone. The monster quickly fled.

The man safely reached the boat on the other side of the loch. He rowed it back. This was the first record of a Loch Ness monster story.

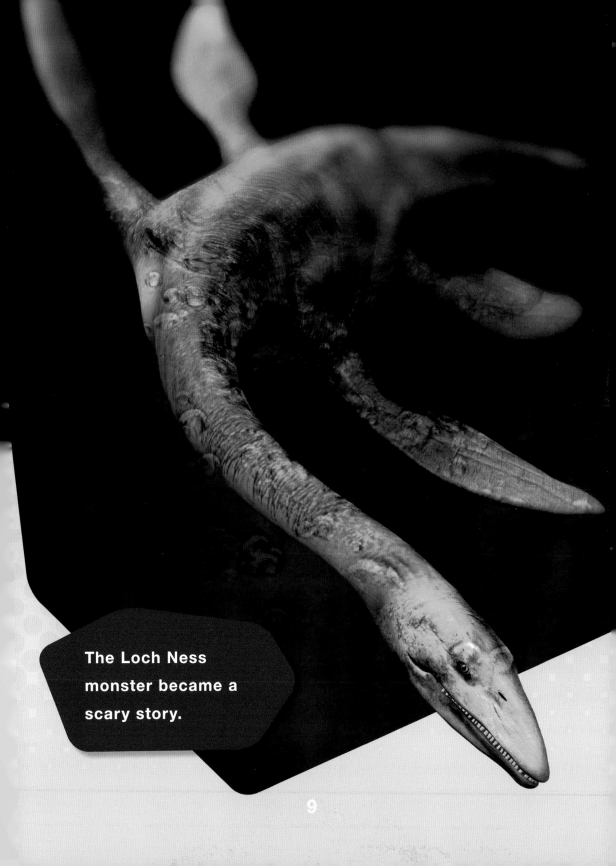

The Loch Ness monster became a scary story.

CHAPTER 2

INTEREST
Grows

The Loch Ness monster is also nicknamed "Nessie". It grew famous around the world in 1933. A couple went by the lake and said they saw a huge monster cross the road. It was 8 metres (25 feet) long. Newspapers told their story.

A sighting in 1938 supposedly shows the Loch Ness monster's shadow (centre).

NESSIE'S FOOTPRINTS

In 1934, the *Daily Mail* newspaper hired a reporter called Marmaduke Wetherell to hunt Nessie. He found footprints. He claimed they were from Nessie.

But the footprints turned out to be fake. They were made with a stuffed hippo's foot. Maybe Wetherell faked the prints himself. Maybe he was tricked. No one knows for sure.

Hippos are not found in Scotland, so many people had not seen their footprints before. Many people believed it to be Nessie's footprint.

The first Loch Ness monster photo supposedly showed Nessie's full neck and head. The picture stunned the world.

PHOTO OF NESSIE

Months later, Robert Wilson took a photo of Nessie. The *Daily Mail* printed the photo. It showed a creature sticking out from the water. It had a small head and long neck. People thought it looked like a plesiosaur. This was a water dinosaur that lived long ago. Tourists rushed to the lake. They hoped to see it themselves.

THE SURGEON'S PHOTO

Wilson's photo is called the "Surgeon's Photo". That is because Wilson was a surgeon. He did not want his name on the image.

CHAPTER 3

RECENT
Photos

People searched the loch for years.

Thousands said they saw Nessie. Some

were lawyers. Some were scientists.

People still claim to see Nessie today.

But no one has found proof that it is real.

Boats cruise around Loch Ness to show tourists the loch. Some hope to see a glimpse of Nessie.

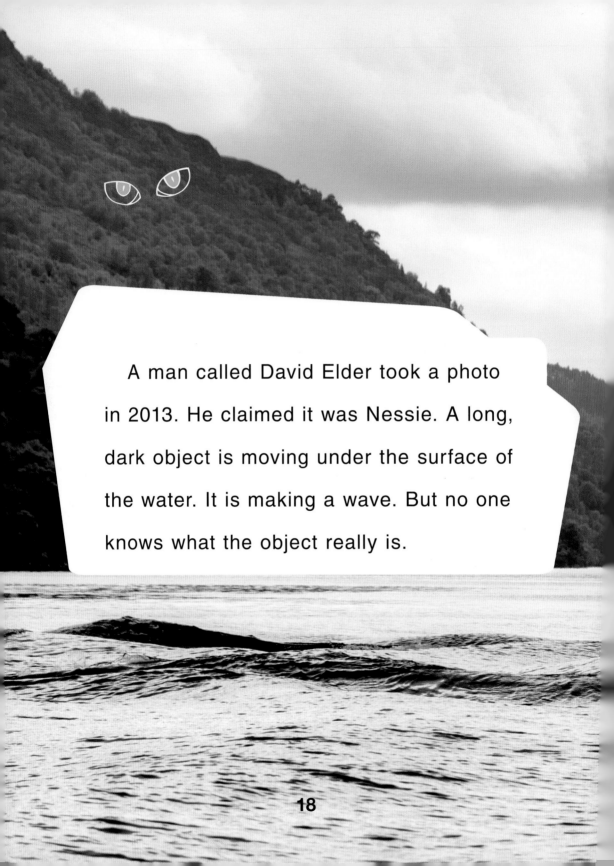

A man called David Elder took a photo in 2013. He claimed it was Nessie. A long, dark object is moving under the surface of the water. It is making a wave. But no one knows what the object really is.

Mysterious waves have been reported in Loch Ness. Some people think the waves could be caused by Nessie moving underneath the surface.

A photo in 2014 also created a lot of interest. Two people were each using a map **app**. They saw something dark on Loch Ness. **Satellites** caught the shadow. It looked like a huge monster. It was 30 metres (100 feet) long. Two flippers came out from its sides. Some people thought it was Nessie. Others said it was just the **wake** of a boat. But a boat was nowhere to be seen.

If Nessie was seen from the satellites, an image above Loch Ness might show a large shadow like this one.

CHAPTER 4

IS NESSIE Real?

In 1994, experts found out that Wilson's 1934 photo was fake. Wetherell and Wilson may have worked together. Wetherell's stepson claimed that the photo was of a toy submarine not Nessie. It had a fake snake head on top of it.

Wetherell was angry with the *Daily Mail* at the time. The newspaper had run stories that made him look bad. This was after he had found the fake footprints. He may have used the photo to get back at the newspaper.

Many people have created fake photos and drawings of Nessie since the 1950s.

People bring their cameras to try to get a photo of Nessie in Loch Ness.

SEARCHING FOR NESSIE

Some people say Nessie photos are easy to explain. Birds and fish can be mistaken for Nessie. So can floating trees.

Yet about 1 million people still visit Loch Ness each year, hoping to spot the water monster. They believe Nessie hides beneath the waves.

The mystery of the
Loch Ness monster will
always be a great story.

NESSIE TODAY

People all over the world enjoy stories of Nessie. It is talked about in many books. *Breaking Dawn* in the Twilight series is one. Nessie is also in many films. One *Scooby-Doo* film is all about the monster. Nessie will continue to interest people for many years.

GLOSSARY

app
an application made for a smartphone

loch
Scottish word for lake

monk
a man who belongs to a religious order

satellite
a spacecraft that circles a larger object in space; satellites gather and send information

wake
ripples of water caused by a moving boat

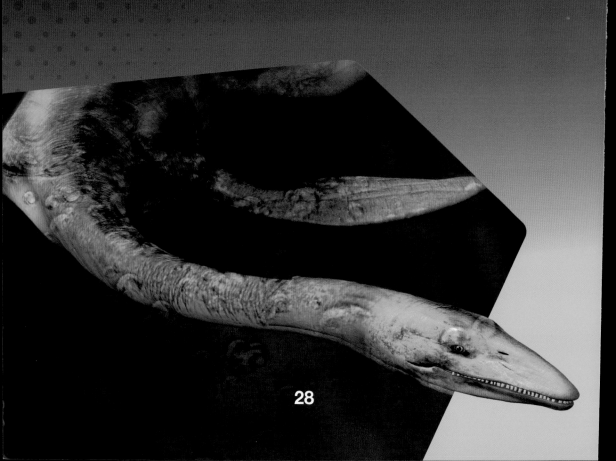

TRIVIA

1. A man named Steve Feltham has made the Guinness Book of World Records for hunting Nessie. He has looked for the Loch Ness monster for the longest number of continuous years. Feltham has been searching for Nessie since 1991.

2. It is believed that Plesiosaurs died out about 80 million years ago. They had a long neck, four fins and a short tail.

3. The name Nessie means "pure".

ACTIVITY

Imagine you are searching for the Loch Ness monster. What do you think you would need? Would you search from a boat or aeroplane? What sort of technology would you use? If you thought you had found evidence, would you share it with the world? Or would you keep it to yourself? Write a paragraph explaining your approach.

FIND OUT MORE

Want to find out more about the Loch Ness monster? Check out these resources:

National Geographic: Loch Ness Monster hoax video
video.nationalgeographic.com/video/loch-ness-sci

The Loch Ness Monster (Autobiographies You Never Thought You'd Read!),
Catherine Chambers (Raintree, 2016)

Curious about Scotland? Learn about this amazing country with these sources:

Scotland (Countries Around the World), Melanie Waldron (Raintree, 2012)

National Geographic Kids: fabulous facts about Scotland!
www.natgeokids.com/za/discover/geography/countries/facts-about-scotland

Visit Scotland: Loch Ness
www.visitscotland.com/destinations-maps/loch-ness

INDEX